ALSO BY LOUIS BAUM

I want to see the moon
Illustrated by Niki Daly
(Shortlisted for the 1985 Best Books for Babies Award)

For Simon and Liz

British Library Cataloguing in Publication Data is available
ISBN 0–370–30692–9

Text copyright © Louis Baum 1986
Illustrations copyright © Paddy Bouma 1986
The Bodley Head Ltd,
First published 1986
Reprinted 1993 by The Bodley Head Children's Books
Random House, 20 Vauxhall Bridge Road, London SW1V 2SA
Random House Australia (Pty) Limited
20 Alfred Street, Milsons Point, Sydney
New South Wales 2061, Australia
Random House New Zealand Limited
18 Poland Road, Glenfield,
Auckland 10, New Zealand
Random House South Africa (Pty) Limited
PO Box 337, Bergvlei 2021, South Africa
Random House UK Limited Reg. No. 954009
Printed and bound in Belgium by Proost International Book Production

Louis Baum

Are we nearly there?

Illustrated by Paddy Bouma

THE BODLEY HEAD

London

Simon and Dad are sailing their boat
in the park on Sunday afternoon.
Round and round the boat goes, round
the sunny pond.
"It's late," says Dad. "It's time to go."
"One more time," says Simon.
"One more time," says Dad.

One more time the boat goes round.
"One more time," says Simon.
"Time to go," says Dad.

Boots, coat, bag, boat, book, picnic and buggy.

"All together and ready to go?"

"Ready to go," says Simon.

"Let's be off then," says Dad.

"Can I have a balloon, Dad? A red one, please?"

"One balloon, a red one, please," says Dad.

Boots, coat, bag, boat, book, picnic,
buggy and balloon.
"All together and ready to go?"
"Ready to go," says Simon.

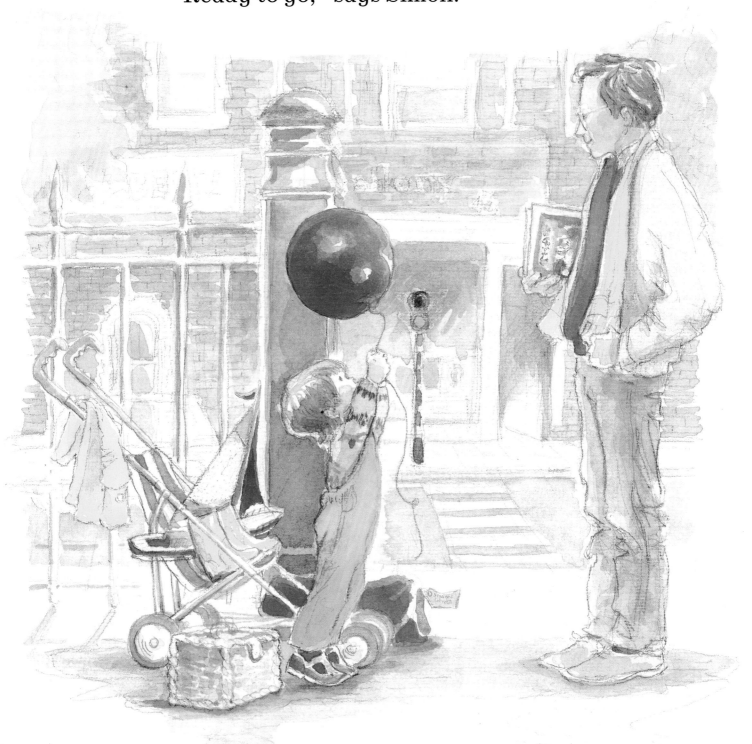

"Return ticket for one, please."
"Can I have a ticket too, please, Dad?"
"You're still too tiny to need a ticket."
"Why am I still too tiny, Dad?"
"Well you're not really too tiny. You're getting bigger every day."

The train is waiting on Platform 9.
"Is it going soon?" asks Simon.
"Any minute now," says Dad.

Slowly the train pulls out of the station.
Along the track there are old buildings,
empty on Sunday afternoon.
"Are we nearly there?" asks Simon.
"We've hardly even started," says Dad.

Now there are houses along the track, each
with a little garden and a little garden shed.
And there are washing-lines and people,
and chimneys in a row, and old cars lying
on bricks.

"Is it very far?" asks Simon.

"Not very far," says Dad.

Then the countryside begins. There are
fields and farms with cows and tractors, and
trees and winding country roads, and the
sun is setting over them through the clouds.

"Are we nearly there?" asks Simon.
"Still a little way to go," says Dad.
"It isn't very far, is it, Dad?" asks Simon.
"No, not very far."

"Shall I read you a story from your book?"
"I'm hungry," says Simon.
"Let's have a picnic instead then," says Dad.
"Oh yes, let's have a picnic."

"One more tomato," says Simon.
"No more tomatoes," says Dad.

Trees and tractors and sleepy cows, and
the sun going down over a hill.

"Shall I read you a story now?" asks Dad.

"Yes, please," says Simon.

"Once upon a time in a distant land, so
far away that most people didn't know
where it was . . ."

"Is it very far?" asks Simon.

"Not very far," says Dad.

"Please will you read the story
one more time?" asks Simon.
"One more time," says Dad.

"Who can see it first?" asks Dad.
"I can see it first!" says Simon.
Behind the hill is a little town. Its lights
are beginning to twinkle.

"Are we nearly there?" asks Simon.
"Nearly there," says Dad.
Slowly the train comes into the station
and stops.

"Now for a little walk," says Dad.
"It isn't very far, is it, Dad?" asks Simon.
"Not very far at all," says Dad.
"Are we nearly there?" asks Simon.
"Nearly there," says Dad.

"Who can see it first?" asks Dad.

"I can see it first!" says Simon.

Around the corner is a dark street and a house with bright lights in the windows.

"We're nearly there," says Simon.

"Nearly there," says Dad.

Boots, coat, bag, boat, book, buggy and balloon.

"All together?"

"All together. Lift me up so I can ring the doorbell, Dad."

"One more time," says Simon.
"Once is quite enough."

"One more hug," says Simon.
"One more hug," says Dad.

"Hello, Simon."
"Hello, Mum."

"Good-bye, Simon."
"Good-bye, Dad."

"See you soon."
"See you soon."